Dragon's Lair

S0-ARC-039

HIRO'S QUEST™
Dragon's Lair

by Tracey West

Illustrated by Craig Phillips

Scholastic Inc.

New York   Toronto   London   Auckland

Sydney   Mexico City   New Delhi   Hong Kong

For Bill,
the Okuno to my Kotone.
— T. W.

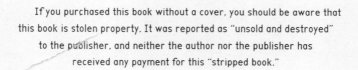

If you purchased this book without a cover, you should be aware that
this book is stolen property. It was reported as "unsold and destroyed"
to the publisher, and neither the author nor the publisher has
received any payment for this "stripped book."

No part of this publication may be reproduced, stored in a retrieval system,
or transmitted in any form or by any means, electronic, mechanical, photocopying,
recording, or otherwise, without written permission of the publisher. For information
regarding permission, write to Scholastic Inc., Attention: Permissions Department,
557 Broadway, New York, NY 10012.

ISBN 978-0-545-21477-3

Text copyright © 2010 by Pure West Productions, Inc.
Illustrations copyright © 2010 by Scholastic Inc.
All rights reserved. Published by Scholastic Inc.
SCHOLASTIC, APPLE PAPERBACKS, HIRO'S QUEST, and associated logos are
trademarks and/or registered trademarks of Scholastic Inc.

12 11 10 9 8 7 6 5 4 3 2 1   10 11 12 13 14 15/0

Printed in the U.S.A.   40
First printing, August 2010
Book design by Jennifer Rinaldi Windau

Chapter One

It was a lazy summer day in Hissori Village, and Hiro Hinata was feeling the heat. Sweat poured down his face as he climbed up a winding mountain path with his friends Aya and Yoshi.

"I can't believe how hard Mr. Sato worked us today," Yoshi complained. He was the shortest of the three friends, with silver-white hair and bright blue eyes.

"We're training to be ninja, Yoshi. It's not supposed

to be easy," Aya pointed out. She had tied her shiny black hair into a ponytail to try to beat the heat.

"But it's not supposed to be torture, either!" Yoshi cried. "Climb that tree! Lift those rocks! Practice those kicks!"

Hiro pressed his palms together and bowed slightly, doing his best impression of their teacher. "Patience, my young student. Without practice, you will never become a rabbit and will remain a fluffy bunny forever."

Aya laughed. Every ninja had the ability to transform into the animal spirit that dwelled inside them. Yoshi's had turned out to be a rabbit.

"Hey, I'm not fluffy!" Yoshi protested.

"Well, actually, you kind of are," Aya told him.

Hiro nodded. "She's right."

Yoshi frowned. "Sure. Just because you have scales, you think you're so cool, Aya."

"Cold-blooded, actually," Aya said with a grin.

As they approached the top of the path leading into Hissori Village, loud voices floated toward them.

"Please! You must believe me! I am not a spy!"

Hiro and his friends raced up the rest of the path to see Hiro's brothers, Kenta and Kazuki, ushering an older man through the village. Each boy held one of the man's arms.

"What are you doing?" Hiro called out.

"Our duty as guardians of Hissori Village," Kazuki said boastfully. He looked bigger and stronger than his seventeen years, and the smaller man in his grasp looked terrified.

"We caught him trying to enter the village," explained Kenta. The middle Hinata brother was two years younger and a head shorter than Kazuki, but just as intimidating with his wiry body and spiked blue hair.

Aya's green eyes narrowed. "How do you know he's not just visiting?"

"He says he's from Gado Village," Kazuki said with a snort. "I've never heard of it."

"Maybe it's far away," Hiro suggested.

"We can't be too careful," Kazuki replied. "Fujita

may have sent him to steal the amulets. He could be a powerful ninja. Or a demon in disguise."

The Hinata family was charged with guarding the Amulet of the Moon and the Amulet of the Sun. The evil ninja Fujita wanted them for himself, to gain ultimate power over the kingdom.

Aya nodded toward the stranger. "Then why hasn't he attacked you?" she asked.

"Listen to her," the man said. "Fujita is why I am here. You see—"

"Aha!" Kazuki boomed. "You are a spy after all! I knew it."

"That's not what he—" Hiro began, but Kazuki and Kenta had already started dragging the poor man up the path.

"Your brother's head is as hard as a rock," Aya remarked to Hiro.

"Yeah, but he sure is tough," said Yoshi. "If I needed protection, Kazuki is the guy I'd ask."

"We'd better follow them," Hiro said.

Kazuki and Kenta dragged the man to the Hinata

house and ushered him inside. Their parents, Rino and Yuto, had been talking quietly in the small dining room, but the commotion coming toward them brought their conversation to a halt.

"This man is a spy for Fujita!" Kazuki announced.

Their mother, Rino, raised an eyebrow. "Really? What did you catch him doing?"

"Walking up to the village gate," Kenta answered. "He looked very suspicious."

"We have many visitors to our gate each day," Yuto pointed out.

"But he knows Fujita! He said it himself!" Kazuki cried. "I tell you, he is a spy!"

"Then why hasn't he attacked you yet?"

Everyone turned to see Mr. Sato standing in the doorway, leaning on his cane. His long, white beard was the same color as his robes.

"That's what *I* asked," Aya muttered.

"Kazuki, Kenta, please let go of this man's arms," Mr. Sato said calmly. "I do not believe he is a danger to us."

Kenta let go right away, but Kazuki hesitated.

"No tricks," he warned the man before loosening his grip.

"Oh, thank you," the man said with relief. He bowed to the group. "I am Mr. Kigi. I come from Gado Village in the Hayashi Valley."

"I traveled through the Hayashi Valley many years ago," said Mr. Sato. "Your homeland is very beautiful."

"See, Kazuki? It's real," Yoshi pointed out helpfully. Kazuki just glared at him.

Mr. Kigi nodded. "We are known for our lush forests and the woodland creatures that live there," he said. "But lately a strange animal has been sighted—a dragon."

Hiro gasped in surprise. He knew only one ninja who could transform into a dragon.

"Is it Fujita?" he asked.

"No one is sure, but that is what many believe," Mr. Kigi replied. "There are rumors in our valley that the members of the Hinata family have defeated Fujita before. I have traveled many days to find you."

"And we will do what we can to help you," said Hiro's mother, Rino. "I apologize for my sons. They did not mean to dishonor you. Please understand that they know the reach of Fujita's evil all too well."

"They are forgiven," Mr. Kigi said kindly. "And I thank you for your offer of help."

"Can you describe the dragon your villagers have seen?" Mr. Sato asked.

Mr. Kigi frowned. "I am afraid we have only glimpsed it. The gleam of an eye. The swish of a long tail. A flash of gold in the darkness. One man said he saw something swimming near the shores of the Jade Lake."

Mr. Sato suddenly looked very excited. "The Jade Lake, you say?"

He turned to Hiro's father. "Yuto, I would ask you to give Mr. Kigi hospitality tonight. In the morning, I will return with him to his village."

"You must let us go with you," Rino said.

Mr. Sato nodded. "I will need ninja to accompany

me." He bowed. "And while it is always an honor to travel with you, the three ninja I would like to take with me are Hiro, Aya, and Yoshi."

Chapter Two

"But they're not even twelve yet!" Kazuki protested. "You should take me and Kenta!"

"I am afraid I must agree," said Rino. "Perhaps you would be better off with more experienced ninja."

Mr. Sato bowed respectfully. "I understand your concern," he said. "However, I do not believe this dragon is Fujita. Kazuki and Kenta are needed here to help you protect the amulets. And this journey will be educational for Hiro, Aya, and Yoshi as a part of their training."

Rino looked at her husband, worried.

"This is not the first time the children have journeyed alone with Mr. Sato," Yuto reminded her.

Rino sighed. "Very well. I, too, went on many journeys as a young ninja. Sometimes it is easy to forget those days."

"We'll be fine," Hiro said.

Rino still looked worried. "You are still my son, Hiro, and I worry about you."

"I will do my best to keep them safe," Mr. Sato said. "And if my suspicions are correct, then the children will not be in any danger."

"What do you mean?" Yoshi piped up. "And how do you know this dragon is not Fujita?"

Mr. Sato just smiled. "Go, and prepare," he said. "We will be gone for many days. And we leave at sunrise."

Aya frowned. "Why does it always have to be sunrise?" she muttered.

Hiro didn't mind leaving at sunrise at all. He would have left that second if it meant getting an answer to the question spinning around in his mind.

If the dragon in the lake wasn't Fujita, then who—or what—was it?

"Welcome to Gado village," said Mr. Kigi with a bow.

"Finally!" Yoshi cried.

"Come on, Yoshi, it wasn't that bad," Aya said. "It only took nine days."

"Easy for you to say. You slithered most of the way here," Yoshi replied. "My feet hurt!"

"I thought rabbits' feet were supposed to be lucky!" Hiro joked.

The nine days had passed slowly for Hiro, but not because he was tired. He was anxious to get to Gado Village and find the dragon. Along the way, they'd seen many interesting sights: strange flowers the color of the rising sun, rocks that looked like sleeping monsters, a swimming hole that looked impossibly deep and cool. But Hiro was always thinking about the adventure ahead.

And now they were finally here. Gado Village was surrounded by thick woods on three sides. The wooden cottages looked similar to the homes in Hissori Village, although the land was flat instead of sloped and steep. Mr. Kigi led them to a pleasant-looking cottage with a stand of berry bushes in front and a wire pen on the side, occupied by one peaceful cow. As they approached, the door flew open and a woman ran outside, followed by three children.

"Benjiro, you're home!" she cried. She and the children threw their arms around him, practically knocking him to the ground.

Mr. Kigi laughed. "I have missed you so!" he said. He picked up the youngest child, a chubby boy who looked about three years old. "Have you been a good boy?"

"Yes, Papa," the boy said.

"I traveled far to find ninja who will search for

the dragon," Mr. Kigi said. "Please welcome our guests."

Mr. Kigi's children hadn't noticed Hiro and the others before; now they stared at them, wide-eyed.

"Are you really ninja?" asked the oldest, a girl.

Hiro nodded. "I am Hiro Hinata, and these are my friends Aya and Yoshi, and our sensei, Mr. Sato."

Mr. Kigi then introduced his wife, Mori, and three children: Matsu, a seven-year-old girl; Rinji, a five-year-old boy; and Mikio, the youngest.

Mrs. Kigi bowed. "Welcome to our home," she said. "You must share our supper."

They followed her into a room with a long wooden dining table. Mrs. Kigi quickly set the table with plates and bowls. She couldn't have known they were coming, yet there was enough bread and soup for all of them—including Yoshi, who had thirds of everything.

The Kigi children were full of questions.

"Can you turn into an animal?"

"How high can you kick?"

"Did you ever turn invisible?"

Hiro and his friends happily answered them. It made Hiro feel like an important, experienced ninja rather than the eleven-year-old ninja-in-training his brothers always reminded him that he was. When the meal was finished, they all helped to clear the table.

"The sun is setting," Mrs. Kigi said. "I will set up sleeping quarters for you."

"There will be no need," said Mr. Sato, standing up. "Mr. Kigi has told us that the dragon is often spotted at night. We must begin our search."

"Really?" Hiro asked, surprised. "We don't have to wait until tomorrow?"

"You have traveled such a long way," Mrs. Kigi said. "Surely you need some rest."

Aya yawned at the mention of the word "rest." But Mr. Sato was not swayed. In fact, Hiro thought he seemed unusually excited.

"Thank you for your hospitality," Mr. Sato said. "We will return when we have news to report."

The Kigi children looked disappointed but were too polite to complain. Instead, they all bowed.

"Good luck, ninja," Matsu said solemnly.

The sky was streaked with orange as they headed into the forest. They didn't get far before the trees seemed to close in around them. It was difficult to see in the dim light, and Hiro knew soon it would get even darker.

"Mr. Sato, we didn't bring any lanterns," Hiro said.

"If we had lanterns, the dragon would see us and hide," the teacher responded. "Our eyes will adjust to the darkness well enough to see our way."

"But it will be difficult to spot the dragon in the dark," Aya pointed out.

Mr. Sato nodded at her. "You know what to do."

Aya closed her eyes and concentrated. Then a shimmering green light surrounded her body. She transformed into a snake with shiny green scales.

"I have excellent night vision," she said. "It comessss with being a sssssnake."

"Cool!" Yoshi said.

"Ssssomebody should pick me up," Aya said. "Then I can lead the way."

Hiro picked up Aya. She wrapped her long body around his arms.

"Thanksss, Hiro."

"No problem," Hiro replied.

They quietly made their way through the forest. Aya warned them about low-hanging tree branches and rocks.

"So we're just supposed to walk around until we find the dragon?" Yoshi asked after a while, in a loud whisper.

"We are heading east, toward the lake," Mr. Sato replied. "I believe that is where we will find her."

Her. So Mr. Sato thought the dragon was female. Hiro wanted to ask him about it but knew he'd only receive some mysterious answer.

He was still lost in thought when he heard Aya cry out.

"Hiro, look out!"

Chapter Three

Something brushed past Hiro's face. Startled, he dropped Aya and transformed into a monkey without even thinking about it. He jumped to the nearest tree branch and grabbed it, ready to launch after his attacker.

Then he saw it—a harmless fruit bat chasing moths through the trees. Hiro suddenly felt embarrassed.

"Sssorry, Hiro," Aya said. "Falssse alarm."

"And I'm sorry I dropped you," Hiro said. He jumped down, transforming back to his human form as he landed. "I thought we were in danger."

"A good ninja reacts quickly, but not without thought," Mr. Sato said gently. "Transforming into your animal form may not always be the best reaction to an attack. You must quickly assess the situation to take the proper action."

"I guess I still have a lot to learn," Hiro admitted.

"A ninja never stops learning," Mr. Sato said. "Every experience we have is a lesson."

Hiro was still embarrassed, but Mr. Sato's words made him feel a little better, and he reached for Aya.

"I won't drop you again," he promised.

"It'sss okay," she said. "It doesssn't hurt."

They walked on . . . and on . . . and on. The deep black, star-filled sky peeked through openings in the tree branches. Occasionally, a shaft of moonlight would make its way through.

Gradually, the trees began to thin out. Yoshi

sniffed the air, his nose twitching.

"I smell water," he said.

Mr. Sato nodded. "Very good, Yoshi. The lake is not far."

Soon the ground beneath their feet turned soft and sandy. They emerged from the thick forest onto the shores of a calm, wide lake. The night air felt cool on their skin.

Moonlight shone on a temple that rose from the lake's center. The walls of the temple glowed a soft green in the moonlight, and Hiro realized they must be made of jade. A jade temple in the Jade Lake.

"It'ssss beautiful," Aya said.

"Yes," Mr. Sato agreed. "The Jade Temple. Legend says that the health of the land is stored inside this temple. If the temple falls, the land will die."

Aya looked up at Hiro. "Pleassse put me down. I'd like to change back now."

"Sure," Hiro said. He gently placed her on the sandy ground. A few seconds later, Aya stood in front of him.

"Night vision is cool," she said. "But it's a little weird. I've got to see this with my own eyes."

"Look!" Yoshi cried out. "The water is stirring!"

It was true. Ripples danced across the lake's surface. Hiro held his breath as something dark began to emerge from the water.

It was a head—a dragon's head with a long snout and large eyes. Shimmering gold scales covered its head and neck.

The three young ninja were frozen in wonder, but Mr. Sato slowly walked up to the edge of the shore.

"Kotone, is that you?" he asked.

Chapter Four

"Okuno?" the dragon replied, calling Mr. Sato by his former name. Her voice was deep but melodious, with tones that reminded Hiro of ringing bells. "Is that you? How long has it been?"

"It is I," Mr. Sato said. "And it has been a very long time indeed."

The dragon swam to shore, and Hiro realized to his surprise that he was not afraid. Fujita, the evil ninja, was terrifying in his dragon form, with fierce fangs and eyes that burned with fiery hate. But this dragon's eyes were blue-green, like the waters of the lake, and filled with kindness.

"Why have you come?" Kotone asked.

"Fujita's quest for power has grown," Mr. Sato explained. "And when nearby villagers caught glimpses of a dragon, they feared Fujita was rising. But I suspected otherwise. Why have you awakened, Kotone?"

"Fujita," the dragon answered. "Although I was sleeping deeply under the waters of the lake, I could sense his power growing. I fear we will battle once more."

"Then we will help you," Mr. Sato said.

Kotone nodded toward the young ninja. "And your friends? What do they know?"

"We don't know anything," Yoshi piped up.

The dragon seemed to smile. "Then I shall tell you my story. But not here. We must seek the safety of the temple. Please, climb on my back."

Kotone turned so they could climb aboard. Then

she slowly and gracefully swam to the temple in the center of the lake, walked up the temple steps, and stepped through the wide entrance.

Hiro and the others jumped off of her back. The main room of the temple was large and mostly empty, but the walls were carved with intricate images of trees, flowers, rivers, lakes, and all kinds of wild creatures.

"This temple's even more beautiful inside," Aya said.

The dragon slowly nodded her large head.

"The Jade Temple embodies the health and beauty of the land. I am its guardian, and have been for years," Kotone said. "But it has not always been this way. Once, I was a young girl, like you." She nodded at Aya.

"What happened?" Aya asked.

"Please, sit and be comfortable," Kotone said. "This story cannot be told quickly."

Mr. Sato rested in the crook of the dragon's leg, and Hiro and the others sat cross-legged on pillows

that lined the smooth jade floor, as Kotone began
her story.

Many years ago, a traveling fortune-teller came to
my parents' village. The fortune-teller told them that
their child would have great power, a power strong
enough to protect the kingdom from all harm.

My parents had only one child at the time, my
brother, Fujita, who was then three years old. They
loved and adored their firstborn son. But they were
poor, and knew Fujita would have to work in the fields
if he lived with them. So they sent Fujita to live with
an important man, a sorcerer named Rai, hoping the
sorcerer could show Fujita how to use his power. They
thought the sorcerer could give my brother what they
could not.

But they were wrong. Rai was not a bad man, but
the only thing he had ever loved was knowledge. He
did not know how to raise a child. He taught Fujita
everything he knew but gave him no love or guidance.

I was born a few years later. In those days—and even today, I am sad to say—the birth of a daughter was not considered as important as the birth of a son. My parents never dreamed that I could be the child in the fortune-teller's prediction. So I worked in the fields along with my parents. But I was happy. They gave me all their love and attention.

Then, when I was nine, a ninja from a neighboring village invited me to train with his students. My parents were surprised. They did not believe a girl could become a ninja. But the sensei convinced them, and they released me to his training. There I met Okuno, another student. We spent many years together learning the ways of the ninja.

Over time, my brother and I both discovered that our animal spirits were dragons. We both grew up to be strong and powerful. Fujita learned great magic, and I became a master ninja. Our skills were meant to save the land, as the fortune-teller had predicted. But because Fujita grew up without love, he became twisted by power and greed.

My brother wanted to become ruler of all of Kenkoro. When I was twenty-one, I learned that he'd plotted to destroy the guardian dragon of the Jade Temple. He wanted to bleed the land of its health and beauty for his own gain. He thought that by controlling the land, he could control everyone in the kingdom.

I did not want to battle my own brother, but I had no choice. I fought side by side with the guardian dragon. During the battle, Fujita struck the guardian dragon with a fatal blow. Before she died, however, she transferred her power to me—the power that connected her to the temple and the land. This extra power allowed me to defeat my brother, and he fled the temple in fear.

The Jade Temple was safe. But when I accepted the guardian dragon's powers, I lost the ability to transform back into my human form. I also accepted the responsibility of guarding the temple. And so I have stayed hidden here, in the waters of the lake, for many years.

"So Fujita is your brother," Hiro said in the wake of the hushed silence following Kotone's story.

"Who's Okuno?" Yoshi asked.

Aya rolled her eyes. "That was Mr. Sato's name before he went into hiding to protect the amulets. Don't you remember?"

Yoshi shrugged. "It's hard for me to remember everything."

Mr. Sato faced Kotone now.

"I should have been fighting by your side," he said, and Hiro noticed a sadness in his voice that he had never heard before. "I am so sorry. I was on a mission. I couldn't reach you in time."

"You must not apologize, Okuno," Kotone said. "This was my destiny. What has happened is what was meant to be."

But something was worrying Hiro. "Do you really think Fujita is going to attack the temple again?" he asked. "Because we battled him, and I used the Amulet of the Sun against him. We don't think he can turn into a dragon anymore."

"Fujita may seem weak, but he is stronger than you realize," Kotone replied. "I would not have awakened otherwise."

Suddenly, Yoshi's ears began to twitch.

"Something's coming," he said.

Hiro and his friends raced to the temple entrance. Four owls came flying toward the temple, their yellow eyes glowing in the darkness.

Hiro remembered Mr. Sato's advice and tried to think before he reacted. The four owls could just be owls—but he knew that Fujita controlled many ninja who could transform into birds.

The owls had brown feathers, and wingspans that looked to be at least eight feet long. They screeched as they dove out of the sky, aiming right for the temple entrance.

"We're under attack!" Hiro yelled.

Chapter Five

Two of the owls transformed into ninja and landed at the temple entrance. They wore all black, including face masks that covered everything except their eyes.

"Get them!" one of the ninja called out, and Hiro was surprised to hear a female voice; Fujita's other minions had all been men.

The other two owls flew at Kotone. The dragon roared, swiping at the owls with her sharp claws.

One of the birds slammed into the temple wall, transforming as she fell to the floor. She cradled her right arm, which hung limply by her side. The remaining owl swooped down, sharp talons extended. Kotone swatted at the bird with her long dragon's tail.

One of the ninja attacked Hiro, spinning and then delivering a sharp kick into Hiro's chest. Hiro fell against the jade floor but quickly pushed himself back up with his hands, kicking his attacker across the backs of her knees.

At the same time, the other ninja aimed a kick at Aya, who grabbed on to her leg and flipped right over it. The ninja turned quickly, grabbed Aya's arms, and held them behind her back. Mr. Sato appeared behind the ninja, whacking her across the back with his walking stick. The ninja cried out in surprise and released Aya.

Hiro's attacker jumped to her feet and began pummeling Hiro in the chest.

"***Aaaaaayaaaaaa!***" Yoshi yelled. He jumped up

in the air, twisting his body and reaching out with his leg to kick the ninja. But the skilled attacker grabbed Yoshi's leg with her right hand while pushing Hiro against the wall of the temple with her left arm.

Hiro was surprised at the ninja's strength. He tried to quickly calculate the best way to get out of her grasp. Then he heard Kotone cry out.

"Move out of the way!"

The dragon charged the temple entrance. She grabbed a ninja in each claw and tossed the two of them into the waters of the lake.

"Aaaaaiiiieeeeeee!"

The last ninja still in owl form cried out in fury and landed on Kotone's back, plucking off some of her gold scales. Kotone twisted her snakelike body around to stop her, but the owl moved quickly. She picked up her injured companion in her claws and fled the temple, flying off into the night.

"Is everyone all right?" Mr. Sato asked.

Hiro took a deep breath. He was a little sore but not seriously hurt.

"I'm okay," he reported.

"Girl ninja are pretty tough," Yoshi remarked.

"Of course we are," Aya snapped.

Mr. Sato examined Kotone's back. "Four scales are missing."

"I don't understand," Hiro said. "Did Fujita send those ninja? Why would he send only four ninja to fight you? There's no way they could win."

"Fujita got what he wanted," Kotone replied.

"You mean the scales?" Aya asked.

Kotone nodded. "That is the only explanation. Dragon scales are a powerful magical ingredient in the potions of sorcerers."

Yoshi looked confused. "I don't get it. Why does Fujita need a potion?"

"I think I can answer that," Mr. Sato replied. "When Hiro defeated Fujita, he lost his ability to turn into a dragon. Perhaps this potion will restore his powers."

Hiro understood. "And if he can turn back into a dragon, he's dangerous again, right?"

Mr. Sato nodded. "Exactly."

"Then we've got to stop him!" Hiro cried.

Kotone turned and moved to a pillar against the back of the temple wall. With her claw, she took a small wand of jade from the top of the pillar and held it out to Mr. Sato.

"Take this," she said. "It will guide you to my dragon scales. You must retrieve them before Fujita can use them."

Mr. Sato took the wand. "I will return. I promise," he said, looking into Kotone's eyes.

"Uh, we'll *all* return, won't we?" Yoshi asked.

"We can't return until we leave," Aya pointed out. "We'd better hurry."

Kotone nodded. "I will take you back to shore."

They climbed onto the dragon's back once more. Mr. Sato held out the jade wand, turning it in all directions until it began to glow with a soft green light.

"We will head north," Mr. Sato said.

When they reached the shore, they said good-bye to Kotone.

"Be careful," she warned. "My brother is very dangerous."

"Oh, we know that," Hiro assured her.

Kotone looked at him, and her blue-green eyes seemed as deep as the ocean.

"Trust me, you don't."

Chapter Six

They followed the trail of the owl ninja all night.
As the sun began to rise, Hiro felt he was fighting
exhaustion with each step he took. He wasn't alone.
Aya and Yoshi were yawning and stumbling through
the trees alongside him. Only Mr. Sato didn't seem
affected by the lack of sleep.

"It's too bad we can't fly," Yoshi said, stopping to
yawn and stretch. "Fujita's probably got those scales
by now."

"The potion Fujita needs cannot be made quickly," Mr. Sato pointed out. "We should have time to stop him."

"And what if we're too late?" Aya asked.

Nobody answered. If they *were* too late, and Fujita could turn into a dragon again, there would be no way to fight him. The powerful Amulet of the Sun was back in Hissori Village.

Suddenly, the jade wand began to glow more brightly than before. Mr. Sato stopped.

"We are very close," he said. "We must move with caution."

They followed the wand through a thicket of dense vegetation, which led to a strange-looking circular stone building. Vines crawled up the walls, nearly covering it completely.

"Is it a temple?" Yoshi asked.

"A hideout, more likely," Mr. Sato replied. "And now we must find the entrance."

They made their way around the building. Hiro parted the vines, looking for a way in. Then he spotted it—a door cut into the stone. But there was no doorknob. How did it open?

"Maybe it just needs a push," Yoshi suggested.

Hiro pressed his palms on the cool stone, and the door slid to the side.

"That was easy," Yoshi said.

"Maybe too easy," Hiro said suspiciously.

"Perhaps," agreed Mr. Sato. "But right now, it is our only way inside."

Mr. Sato stepped through the doorway, followed by Hiro and the others. The entrance opened up into a wide square room with no other doors or windows.

"An empty room?" Hiro asked. "This can't be—"

There was a rumbling sound, and the door behind them slid shut. Hiro felt something under his feet and realized it was rising up from the floor, right under his feet.

With a cry, he flipped backward as a wall shot up, slamming into the ceiling and separating him from Mr. Sato, Aya, and Yoshi.

He was alone in a room with no escape.

"Hey!" Hiro yelled, pounding on the walls. "I'm in here!"

He heard muffled cries from the other side, but nothing that made sense. Hiro took a deep breath.

Keep calm, he told himself. *Look for a way out. There's always a way out.*

Hiro stepped away from the wall.

Whoosh! The floor opened up beneath him, and he felt himself fall. Thinking quickly, he transformed into his monkey form and somersaulted as he hit the floor below.

He got to his feet and waited for his eyes to adjust to the darkness. He was in some kind of narrow passageway now. Cautiously, he made his way forward.

The hallway twisted and turned, and Hiro guessed he was in some kind of maze. *But where does it lead?* he thought. *To Fujita? Or to something even worse?*

Finally, he saw a ladder up ahead. Hiro wondered if it led to another trapdoor. He hurried toward the ladder.

But before he could reach it, he heard an unusual sound behind him — a furious whirring. Hiro felt the familiar touch of leathery wings brushing past his face.

He was being pursued by a bat!

His first instinct was to run. But he knew he could not run faster than the bat could fly. The dark creature—was it one of Fujita's ninjas?—flew circles around him, flapping its wings in Hiro's face.

Think, Hiro told himself, trying to remember Mr. Sato's advice. *What can a monkey do to defeat a bat?*

Then something clicked in his mind—something he had learned in school about bats. They targeted their prey using echolocation—bouncing sound waves off of an animal and then following the trail. Like bouncing a ball against a wall and having it bounce back to you.

Hiro knew what to do. He had to make it difficult for the bat to find him. . . .

Using his monkey agility, Hiro dodged left, dodged right, jumped up, jumped down. He ricocheted off of

the walls, propelling himself in different directions with each jump.

The bat kept up at first, but soon it began to fly around erratically. Hiro jumped away from the confused bat, grabbing the rungs of the ladder. Then he pulled himself upward and pushed on the ceiling.

To his relief, a small square of stone swung upward. He quickly climbed through the opening, then closed the door behind him before the bat could follow.

He paused for a moment to catch his breath before getting to his feet.

He had to find his friends. Fast.

Chapter Seven

"Mr. Sato? Hiro? Yoshi?"

Aya's voice echoed off of the stone walls. She had been just as surprised as Hiro when the walls had shifted, separating them from one another.

The walls around Aya formed a passage that got darker and narrower farther down. Aya quickly transformed into a snake, knowing she'd have an advantage in the darkness.

She slithered down the hallway. Creating the

back-and-forth movement of her body was becoming easier each time she transformed. There were times when Aya wished that the snake was her true form. Being a snake was so much simpler than being an eleven-year-old girl.

The hallway opened up into a large room. Aya cautiously poked her head inside to see what waited for her there. Strange symbols were carved into the walls. Stone pillars of various heights were arranged around the otherwise empty room.

Someone could be hiding around one of those pillars, Aya reminded herself. She used her snake senses to feel any body heat emanating from the room, but the stone felt cool.

Cautiously, Aya slithered inside. First she heard a door slide shut behind her, and then she realized she was transforming—against her will.

A hole in the ceiling opened up, and a black-clad ninja jumped down. "No one can transform in this room," the ninja laughed, nodding toward the walls. "It's charmed. Fujita has placed magical charms in every room of this hideout."

At first, Aya thought she recognized the owl ninja she'd battled at the Jade Temple. But from her size and the sound of her voice, Aya realized the ninja was a girl, probably around her own age.

"What do you want?" Aya asked.

The girl backflipped twice, landing on top of one of the stone pillars. She looked down at Aya and grinned behind her mask. Aya could see the smile in her eyes.

"The master has sent me to defeat you," she said.

Aya realized that the only way to get out of the room would be to best the ninja in a battle, and the thought scared her. She had never fought an enemy one-on-one before, except in her training with Hiro and Yoshi. Even then, she always fared better in her snake form.

"Fujita is your master? Then you have learned nothing but bad manners," Aya scoffed. "This is no way to welcome visitors to your home."

The girl jumped off of the pillar. Aya moved to dodge the attack, but the ninja landed a kick on her shoulder. Aya tumbled backward.

She jumped to her feet as the ninja swiped a knife-hand strike to her collarbone, but Aya quickly blocked it with an upraised palm. The ninja didn't let up, delivering another strike with her left hand.

"You're good," Aya said, blocking the blow once again. "Why are you wasting your time serving a creep like Fujita? Didn't your family teach you right from wrong?"

The girl jumped over Aya's head, hoping to surprise her from behind. But Aya whirled around and blocked another blow.

"My family is gone," the girl replied. "Wiped out in a flood in seconds. Right and wrong don't matter much to me."

Aya felt a pang of sympathy for the girl, but she pushed it aside. This was a battle, after all.

The girl stepped up her attack, swiftly alternating hands, hoping Aya couldn't block fast enough.

But Aya could strike as swiftly as a snake, and she could block just as fast. Frustrated, the ninja jumped up on one of the lower pillars, and Aya instinctively jumped onto the pillar next to her.

Immediately, she regretted the move. She had never felt comfortable jumping and climbing; that was Hiro's strength. She preferred to be close to the ground, where she could feel the steady earth beneath her feet. The ninja noticed.

"Too bad you can't fly," the girl taunted her. "This is going to be the easiest test of my skills yet."

She attacked with a roundhouse kick. Aya jumped over it.

"Test, huh? What happens if you fail?" Aya asked. "I'll wager that Fujita won't be understanding."

The ninja's eyes blazed with anger. She delivered another roundhouse kick, stronger than before, and this one nearly knocked Aya off of her feet.

The next thing Aya felt was a sharp kick to her chest. She toppled off of the pillar, reaching out at the last second to block her fall.

The girl ninja laughed. "Come back up here and fight."

She would want that, wouldn't she? Aya realized. *If she's one of those owl ninja, she's probably more comfortable off of the ground.*

"Come and get me," Aya growled.

The ninja's eyes narrowed. She jumped off of the pillar, her right leg extended to deliver another kick. Aya jumped up and grabbed the ninja's ankle before it could make contact. But the girl broke away and quickly resumed an assault of fast knife-hand strikes.

52

Once again, Aya expertly blocked them, but she knew that wasn't good enough to win the battle. She had some strong offensive moves in her arsenal—powerful strikes that could take down an opponent. But she had to get close enough to use them. She needed the element of surprise.

That's it! Aya suddenly realized. She didn't have to use the pillars for aerial moves, like the ninja. She could use them for cover.

Aya quickly ducked, sliding past the ninja on the stone floor. Then she somersaulted and stopped behind one of the pillars.

"You're afraid, are you?" the girl ninja asked. "I'm here to fight, not play hide-and-seek."

Aya didn't take the bait. She waited patiently, controlling her breath so the ninja couldn't hear her.

The girl was good. She moved silently, as a ninja should. Aya closed her eyes, concentrating on her snake energy. Even if she couldn't transform, it was there inside her.

Finally she felt it—the body heat of the ninja as she moved among the pillars, looking for Aya. Aya slowly rose into a crouching position, ready to strike.

Wham! Aya made her move so quickly, the girl ninja had no time to react. Aya pounced, striking the girl in the neck and pinning her to the floor.

"Your master needs to teach you better," Aya said.

Aya swiftly leapt away from the girl and began jumping from one pillar to the next until she reached the hole in the ceiling. She pulled herself up through it, then paused to look down. The ninja lay motionless on the ground, but her eyes were full of fury.

"You'll be able to move in a minute or two," Aya shouted down to her. "If I were you, I'd get out of here and find a new master. Fujita is evil. And something tells me you're better than that."

With that, Aya ran off to find her friends.

Chapter Eight

"Hiro? Is that you?"

Hiro whirled around at the sound of his friend's voice. "Aya!"

Aya ran up to him. "I'm so glad I found you," she said. "I got stuck in a room with a ninja and had to battle her. And I couldn't transform!"

"I guess you won, or you wouldn't be here now," Hiro said. "I had to battle a bat. Then I got out, but this place is like a maze, and I can't figure out where we are. I've been going left and right, up and down."

"Me, too," Aya agreed. "I feel like I've been walking in circles, and I'm not even sure what floor we're on." Then she frowned. "I'm worried about Yoshi."

Hiro nodded. "It's almost like Fujita set this up to separate us, to take us down one by one. But you and I made it, and Mr. Sato can take care of himself. I'm sure Yoshi is okay."

"I hope so," Aya said. "But I'll be happier when we find him—and a way out."

"I've been thinking," Hiro said. "The building is shaped like a circle. So it's easy to get confused and go around and around. We should look for hidden doorways in the walls. They may lead outside."

"Or to more hidden rooms," Aya pointed out. "That's smart, Hiro. Let's try it."

They made their way slowly through the twisting passageways, pressing their palms to the walls as they moved. It didn't take long for them to get results. Hiro soon felt a piece of the wall shift beneath his fingertips.

"I found one!" he cried out.

The door slid to the side, and Hiro and Aya entered a small stone room. There Yoshi lay on the floor, pale and soaked in sweat. They quickly ran to his side.

"Yoshi, are you all right?" Aya asked.

"There was a snake ninja," Yoshi answered in a weak voice. "Not like you, Aya. A scary one. I got bit." He pointed to his right ankle.

Hiro knelt down and examined the ankle. The bite was red and swollen. Aya quickly removed the sash from her tunic.

"Tie this above the bite," she instructed Hiro. "It will help stop the poison from traveling."

She put a hand on Yoshi's shoulder. "Hiro and I are going to get you out of here, okay?"

Yoshi nodded. "Sounds good to me." Then he closed his eyes.

Hiro grabbed Yoshi under one arm, and Aya grabbed the other. Hiro nodded to his friend.

"Let's do it."

They lifted Yoshi to his feet. Thankfully, he was

smaller than either of them and fairly light.

"Now what?" Aya asked.

"We keep moving," Hiro said. "We found this room. I'm sure we can find a way out. We just have to stay calm."

"Calm. Right," Aya said with a nod. "Let's move."

They slowly continued on through the maze, carrying Yoshi and testing the walls for secret doors.

Soon, Aya spoke up. "There's something here," she said. "Should we try it?"

"What choice do we have?" Hiro asked.

Aya pressed on the stone, and the door slid open. When they peered through the doorway, a strange chill came over them. An eerie purple mist filled the room, and they could see only a few feet in front of them. Hiro suddenly felt very afraid.

"I don't like this," Hiro hissed.

"We have to check it out," Aya insisted. "It could be the only way out."

Hiro knew she was right. They slowly stepped

into the room. As they made their way inside, they saw a small round table in the center of the room, topped with a collection of stones and amulets. A glass jar hung suspended in midair above the table, surrounded by the mist. The jar was filled with glowing purple liquid, and something else—four shiny gold dragon scales.

"The scales!" Hiro cried.

Then a voice slid through the mist, a voice as slick as oil.

"Yes, you have found the scales. But you shall not take them."

A tall figure staggered into view. The man was thin, wearing long, purple robes. A pointy black beard covered his narrow chin, and a black mustache drooped down the sides of his mouth. His eyes glowed with an angry fire.

"Fujita," Hiro whispered. He could barely breathe, he was so afraid.

But then he noticed something. He had seen Fujita once before in human form, and this man looked different—thinner, paler, weaker. Aya noticed it, too.

"We passed your little tests, and now we're taking the scales," she said bravely.

Fujita chuckled. "Not all of you passed," he said, eyeing Yoshi. "Your friend here does not have much time. And the man you worship so dearly, your Mr. Sato, is not here to help you, is he?"

Hiro knew Fujita was toying with them, but he couldn't help feeling alarmed. Had something happened to Mr. Sato?

"Besides, those were not tests, my dear girl," Fujita continued. "Just games, for my amusement. Now, this . . . *this* is a test."

Fujita snapped his fingers, and a dozen ninja descended from the ceiling. Hiro and Aya looked at each other and laid Yoshi on the ground. Then they each stood in battle stance.

"You take six and I'll take six, okay?" Hiro joked.

"Betcha I can do eight," Aya shot back.

They sounded confident, but inside they were

both terrified. There was no way they could take on twelve ninja by themselves, and Fujita knew it.

"Attack!" Fujita yelled.

As the twelve ninja landed, Hiro and Aya steeled themselves for the assault.

Then they heard a loud roar, a roar so powerful that it caused the floors to tremble. A look of terror crossed Fujita's face.

Hiro and Aya turned toward the door as a huge red dragon burst into the room.

Chapter Nine

"Grab Yoshi!" Aya yelled over the dragon's roar. Together, she and Hiro quickly pulled him out of the dragon's path.

The ninja descended on the dragon, but they might as well have been flies. The dragon swatted at each of them with his powerful forelegs. Hiro noticed that this dragon looked more like Kotone than Fujita's animal spirit. His body was long and snakelike, and he didn't have wings.

That's when Hiro remembered—the scales!

"I've got to get the dragon scales," he told Aya.

She nodded. "I'll stay with Yoshi."

Hiro quickly transformed into a monkey and jumped over the dragon's back. The dragon appeared to be on their side, but Hiro couldn't be sure. Their best bet was to grab the scales and get out of Fujita's hideout as quickly as possible. Hiro jumped up and grabbed the glass jar floating above the table. He felt a slight tingle as he touched the jar.

Then he felt a hand grab his tail.

"**NO!**" Fujita wailed. Startled, Hiro dropped the jar, and it shattered all over the floor.

Fujita dropped Hiro and bent down to pick up the scales. He grabbed one, but before he could pick up the others, a red claw slammed into the evil ninja.

"Hiro! The scales!" the dragon growled.

Hiro barely had time to register that the dragon's voice sounded familiar before rushing to gather the remaining three scales. He raced back and transformed, putting the scales safely in his pocket.

Behind him, Fujita yelled, "Retreat!"

The few ninja who hadn't been knocked out by the dragon swooped around Fujita and hauled him up through a door in the ceiling.

The dragon glowed with a soft red light as the creature transformed into a human—a man they all knew.

"Mr. Sato!" Hiro cried.

The old man picked up something from the round table and turned to his young students.

"Come," he said. "We must get Yoshi back to Kotone. She can heal him."

Mr. Sato led them out of the maze so smoothly that Hiro wondered if it were mapped in his head. When they got outside, he instructed them to place Yoshi on the ground. Mr. Sato knelt down and examined him, feeling his pulse and listening to his breathing. He frowned.

"What is it?" Aya asked.

"I fear we may not reach the Jade Temple in time to save Yoshi."

"I can help."

They looked up to see a young ninja standing beside them. Aya recognized her voice immediately.

"Who are you?" Hiro asked.

"It's the ninja I fought inside Fujita's lair," Aya said.

The ninja took off her mask. As Aya suspected, she didn't look much older than twelve or thirteen. She had round, brown eyes and wore her sleek brown hair in a ponytail.

"He's light," the girl said. "I can fly him there."

Mr. Sato nodded. "It is his only chance."

"Wait a second!" Hiro protested. "She works for Fujita. We can't trust her with something like this. Yoshi could die!"

The girl bowed her head. "I am Kuro," she said. "I will take good care of your friend. Fujita is no longer my master."

Aya suspected that Kuro hadn't had a choice in the matter. Fujita had probably banished her when she lost to Aya, failing his test. Was this an attempt to get back into Fujita's favor—by delivering Yoshi to him?

Somehow, Aya didn't think so. Something inside—call it intuition, call it her snake-sense—told her that this girl was not a danger.

"It's okay, Hiro," Aya said, fixing her eyes on Kuro. "I trust her."

Hiro was torn. He didn't trust this girl at all—but he knew Yoshi needed help, fast.

"Fine," he said. "Take him."

Kuro transformed into an owl with a magnificent wingspan. She picked up Yoshi by his shirt and carried him over the trees, screeching as she flew off toward the temple.

Hiro broke into a run. "Come on!" he urged. "Yoshi needs us!"

They made their way back to the Jade Temple as quickly as they could. When they got there, they found Kotone waiting for them at the shore.

"Come," she said. "Your friend is inside the temple. He is doing well."

She carried them across the lake on her back. Hiro jumped off first and raced inside. He wouldn't believe Yoshi was all right until he saw his friend with his own eyes.

Yoshi was propped up on a bed of large pillows. His cheeks were pink and his eyes were clear. He looked like his old self.

"Are you okay?" Hiro asked.

"I feel pretty good," Yoshi replied. Then his face clouded. "Just angry at myself, I guess. I should've been able to defeat the ninja that attacked me."

"Yoshi, I couldn't have defeated a poisonous snake," Hiro told him. "I'm just glad you're okay."

He looked around the temple. "Where's Kuro?"

"Who's Kuro?" Yoshi asked.

"The owl ninja who brought you here," Hiro told him.

Yoshi shrugged. "I don't remember anything except waking up here. Kotone said she healed me with a potion she made from water from the lake, but I don't even remember drinking it. Sorry."

Kotone, Aya, and Mr. Sato entered the temple.

"I must thank you all for your brave actions," she said. "I am in your debt."

"You saved our friend," Hiro said. "We are the ones who owe you. Besides, I only got three of the scales back. Fujita still has one."

"Could Fujita use that scale to make another potion?" Yoshi asked.

"I do not know for sure," Kotone said. "And I worry that he will send his ninja to steal more scales. My brother does not give up easily."

"Neither do I," said Mr. Sato. He removed a silver chain from the pouch hanging from his belt. On the chain hung a silver tube with unusual markings. "Fujita had this in his possession."

Kotone's eyes widened. "A Vessel of Holding," she said.

Mr. Sato nodded. "This should allow you to transform back into a human at will," he said. "If you are attacked again, there will be no scales to steal."

As he placed the vessel in Kotone's claw, she closed her eyes.

The transformation happened slowly—Kotone had been a dragon for a very long time. Gold light snaked around her body. She grew smaller. Her scales faded away.

Finally, a woman stood in front of them. She had long, black hair streaked with gray. Blue-green eyes shone from her wrinkled face. She placed the chain around her neck, and then clutched Mr. Sato's hands.

"Okuno," she said. "Thank you."

Mr. Sato looked into her eyes. "Kotone."

Yoshi jumped up from his pillows. "You can come back to Hissori Village with us now, can't you?"

Kotone broke away from Mr. Sato's gaze, shaking her head. "I cannot. Whether human or dragon, I must remain at the temple. I am still its guardian. If the temple falls, the land will die."

Mr. Sato turned to the children. "I shall remain at the temple, too. For a while, at least."

Hiro was confused. "But we need to get home. Fujita's back, and the amulets are—"

Aya nudged him. "Can't you see? They're in love."

Hiro's cheeks flushed. That thought would never have occurred to him in a million years.

"The amulets are in good hands with your family," said Mr. Sato. "I have spent many years in Hissori Village. It is time I took a . . . vacation."

"But what about us?" Yoshi asked. "It's a long journey home."

"One you can handle," said Mr. Sato. "You have proven your worth as ninja many times over."

Yoshi hung his head. "Hiro and Aya have proven themselves," he said. "But not me."

"One defeat does not erase all of your brave actions, Yoshi," Mr. Sato told him. "A true ninja can never experience the joy of victory unless he has experienced the pain of defeat."

Yoshi nodded. "I understand the pain part, all right," he said with a small shudder.

"Besides, you won't be alone this time, Yoshi," Hiro reminded him. "It'll be the three of us."

Yoshi held out his hand. Hiro slapped his hand on top of Yoshi's, and Aya added hers.

"Promise?" Yoshi asked.

"Promise," Hiro and Aya replied.

Chapter Ten

"Did you really ride on a dragon's back?" Matsu asked.

"Children, you ask too many questions," Mrs. Kigi scolded.

"It's okay," Hiro said. "I don't mind."

After saying good-bye to Mr. Sato and Kotone, Hiro, Aya, and Yoshi had made their way back to Gado Village, where Mr. and Mrs. Kigi welcomed them. Then they slept for a very, very long time. Now they were eating a feast provided by Mrs. Kigi and other grateful members of the village.

Hiro had never seen so much food on one table: fragrant bowls of rice, two roast chickens, pots of steaming vegetable soup, plates of pork dumplings. His stomach rumbled at the sight of the feast, as though it suddenly remembered it needed to be fed.

"Hiro, tell us again how you turned into a monkey and fought a bat," Matsu pleaded.

Hiro repeated the tale between bites of food.

Rinji turned to Yoshi. "Did it hurt when you got bit by a snake?"

Yoshi's face was still. He didn't answer. Mrs. Kigi shot Rinji a warning look.

"That is enough questions," she said. "Let our guests eat in peace."

Rinji looked down at his plate. "Sorry, Mama."

Little Mikio made a funny face. "Snakes? Yuck!"

"Not *all* snakes are bad," Aya pointed out, and almost everyone laughed, breaking the tension for a moment.

But Yoshi didn't smile. Hiro could tell that, even though his friend's body was healed, Yoshi was still upset. A wave of anger rose up inside him. Why did Fujita want to hurt others? Why would he sic a poisonous snake on a kid, even if the kid was a ninja? Hiro could never, ever imagine doing that to someone else.

He remembered Kotone's story—how Fujita's loveless, lonely upbringing had left him cold and heartless. Hiro silently thanked his own parents. His older brothers could be hard to live with sometimes, but he'd much rather live with them than an unfeeling sorcerer.

"Mom, can I be a ninja when I grow up?" Matsu asked suddenly.

Mrs. Kigi shook her head and made a clicking noise with her tongue. "That is very dangerous work, Matsu. You would be much happier here in the village. You could become a weaver or a schoolteacher."

"I don't want to do that! I want to fight bad guys, like Hiro and Aya and Yoshi!" Matsu replied.

"We do not know your future, Matsu," Mr. Kigi said gently. "But if you do become a ninja, I hope you will become one with a good heart, like our friends here."

"Me, too!" Matsu said.

Mrs. Kigi insisted that Hiro, Aya, and Yoshi spend another night so they would be well rested for their journey home. They woke to a hearty meal of eggs, hot cereal, and tea.

"There is fresh water in your packs, and rice with leftover chicken for your lunch," she told them. "Please get home quickly and safely."

She hugged Hiro, and for a moment he was reminded of his own mother. He really missed her— and everyone else back in Hissori Village.

"Don't worry," he told her. "We'll head straight home."

Mr. Kigi bowed. "No one in Gado Village will ever forget your courage."

Hiro, Aya, and Yoshi bowed in return.

"And we will never forget your kindness and hospitality," Aya said.

As they said good-bye to the Kigi family and began the long journey home, Matsu, Rinji, and Mikio waved . . . and waved . . . and waved until they were specks in the distance.

"Is it just me, or does it feel weird that Mr. Sato's not here?" Yoshi asked.

"It's definitely weird," Aya agreed. "I hope he'll be home soon."

"Me, too," Hiro agreed.

Yoshi cocked his head. A mischievous glint filled his blue eyes, and Hiro was glad to see it. "So, did you really mean what you said about going straight home?" he asked.

Hiro stopped. "Why?"

"Well, I was just remembering that swimming hole we passed in that village by the waterfall, remember?"

Aya closed her eyes. "Ooh, it looked so nice and cool."

"I'm just saying," Yoshi said. "It might be nice to check it out. So we don't get hot."

Hiro grinned. "That's very smart, Yoshi. Let's do it."

The three young ninja continued on the path, headed for home—and maybe one swimming hole. They had a long journey in front of them, and Hiro didn't know what dangers lay ahead.

To his surprise, that thought didn't scare him as much as it used to. They were ninja, after all. And facing danger was what ninja did.

HIRO'S WORLD

Hiro's Quest is a work of fantasy,
but it is based on some real ideas
and elements from Japan and
other places around the world.

Inside the Jade Temple
A Note from the Author

The temple guarded by Kotone is made entirely of green jade. Jade can come in a variety of colors, but green is the most recognizable. Throughout history, people have believed that jade has special powers. The ancient Aztecs and Mayans made ornaments and amulets from jade.

Jade is especially prized in China. The Chinese believe that jade symbolizes five virtues: kindness, goodness, wisdom, bravery, and purity. More than 5,000 years ago, the Chinese began using jade to make a type of amulet shaped like a flat disc with a hole in the center. These amulets, called *bi*, were said to represent the sun, sky, or heaven. Bi were often found buried with the dead. People thought they would help the dead find their way to heaven. Bi might have also been carried to ward off evil.

Today, jade is used to make all kinds of objects, from jewelry to statues. Sometimes jade is carved into small animals. Each animal is supposed to help the person who carries it. A jade dragon might bring good luck. And someone wanting more courage might carry a jade tiger amulet.

In the story, the walls of the Jade Temple are carved with beautiful images. But it is actually very difficult to carve a hard stone like jade. Today, craftspeople use machines with diamond-tipped points to carve jade. But in ancient China, carving jade took a lot of time and patience because those tools didn't exist. The elaborate carvings in the temple show just how important the temple is. No wonder the Jade Temple needs a powerful, magical guard!

The fate of the kingdom rests in one young ninja's hands....

BEASTQUEST®

→→ THE DARK REALM ←←

FIGHT THE BEASTS,
FEAR THE MAGIC,
IN THIS EXCITING
NEW ADVENTURE!

TORGOR THE MINOTAUR

THE AIR TINGLED AS TOM STEPPED INTO THE Lion's Gate. It had appeared from the lake in Avantia after he had defeated Trillion the evil three-headed lion, but Tom had no idea what lay on the other side.

His horse, Storm, reared up. "Steady, boy," Tom murmured, patting the stallion's glossy neck. Storm rolled his eyes nervously but let Tom lead him forward.

Tom's friend Elenna walked at his side, with Silver close by. The wolf raised his muzzle and whined mournfully.

"We have to do this," Tom muttered through clenched teeth. "Malvel is here somewhere, I know it!"

"You're right, Tom." Elenna's voice was steady. "And we have to rescue Aduro."

Tom stepped out of the gate. A flash of pure white light almost blinded him, and a shudder of energy shot through his body. He stumbled and had to hold on to Storm's reins to keep himself from falling. He heard Elenna cry out in shock, and Silver gave a high-pitched howl.

When Tom's eyes cleared again, he found himself standing in a wasteland. Flat, featureless ground stretched out as far as he could see. A few plants with limp, dark leaves and sprawling stems poked up through the gritty soil, looking as if they were dead or dying. A gnarled tree, bare of leaves, stretched out its twisted branches toward the four friends, and gray clouds hung low beneath a red, swirling sky. In the other direction lay desolate marshes, with reed beds and scum-filled pools. Huge bubbles rose to the surface of the filthy water and burst with a gurgle and a foul smell.

"Ugh!" Elenna choked. "The whole place reeks. Has Malvel poisoned everything?"

Tom shivered and set his teeth against the damp, cold air, while Elenna pulled her shawl out of Storm's saddlebag and drew it tightly around her shoulders. "What place is this?" she asked.

"It is the kingdom of Gorgonia," a stranger's voice said from behind them.

They spun around to see a tall figure dressed in ragged brown robes, standing just in front of the Lion's Gate. Tom reached for his sword. Silver let out a growl from deep inside his throat, and Elenna grasped her bow, taking an arrow from her quiver.

The newcomer leaned on a staff of gnarled wood, staring at them. His head was bald, and one eye was covered by an eye patch; the other eye was a glittering gray.

"Who are you?" Tom asked boldly. He gripped his sword more tightly as the man shuffled forward. "Don't come any closer."

The strange man's mouth twisted in amusement. "Have I frightened you?" He gave a bow. "My name is Kerlo. I am the gatekeeper of Gorgonia."

"Are you a servant to Malvel?" Tom demanded.

"I am not," Kerlo said. "I do not serve any king or wizard. I simply watch the gate."

Tom wasn't sure he could trust this man, but there was no one else to ask for information. "What do you know about Malvel?" he asked. "I have to find him. Does he live near here?"

Again Kerlo let out a short laugh. "Find Malvel? You and your friend should go back to Avantia before it is too late. Gorgonia does not welcome foolish heroes."

"We are no fools. We're here to rescue my friend, the Wizard Aduro," Tom explained.

"And we're not going back until we find him," Elenna added defiantly.

Kerlo smiled, showing two rows of blackened teeth. "Very well, if you insist . . ." He stretched out a hand, pointing across the marshland with a bony finger. "That is the best way forward."

Then dark shadows began to swirl in front of the Lion's Gate, and the mysterious gatekeeper vanished into thin air.

MORE BOOKS!
MORE BEASTS!

- ❏ Beast Quest #1: Ferno the Fire Dragon $4.99 US
- ❏ Beast Quest #2: Sepron the Sea Serpent $4.99 US
- ❏ Beast Quest #3: Cypher the Mountain Giant $4.99 US
- ❏ Beast Quest #4: Tagus the Night Horse $4.99 US
- ❏ Beast Quest #5: Tartok the Ice Beast $4.99 US
- ❏ Beast Quest #6: Epos the Winged Flame $4.99 US
- ❏ Beast Quest #7: Zepha the Monster Squid $4.99 US
- ❏ Beast Quest #8: Claw the Giant Ape $4.99 US
- ❏ Beast Quest #9: Soltra the Stone Charmer $4.99 US

■SCHOLASTIC

SCHOLASTIC and associated logos
are trademarks and/or registered
trademarks of Scholastic Inc.

www.scholastic.com/beastquest

BQBL9